A STAKE IN THE HEART
CAN BE QUITE DISCONCERTING . . .

but Vampires are a Count's best friend. Listen dear reader and you shall learn the moral of the story of Count Alexis: Love is Blind.

And what of Barton Frisbee, artist and window decorator in fashionable downtown Los Angeles? How do you think *he* felt when the mannequin he loved fell for another stiff?

. . . Which brings us, supernaturally, to the subject of baseball widows and their men. Take it from Boris Karloff, *no one* can beat The Graveyard Nine for sheer terror on the diamond.

Speaking of diamonds . . . whatever happened to Astra Vale who made a bargain with the Devil for a face that would drive men mad?

And for unadulterated madness, there's nothing to compare with a boxed-in New Yorker such as Hugo James, who takes comfort from the noises of an unseen neighbor . . . until . . .

(Poor Hugo! Didn't your mother ever tell you, "If you're not expecting company, don't open the door!")

BORIS KARLOFF

presents

TALES OF THE

FRIGHTENED

Text by

MICHAEL AVALLONE

PYRAMID BOOKS ▲ NEW YORK

BORIS KARLOFF PRESENTS TALES OF THE FRIGHTENED

A PYRAMID BOOK

Copyright © 1973 by Pyramid Communications, Inc.
Copyright © 1963 by Lyle Kenyon Engel

Second Printing, December 1973

ISBN 0-515-03282-4

This book is fiction. The characters are fictitious,
and any resemblance to actual persons,
living or dead, is purely coincidental.

Pyramid Books are published by Pyramid Communications, Inc.
Its trademarks, consisting of the word "Pyramid" and the portrayal
of a pyramid, are registered in the United States Patent Office.

Pyramid Communications, Inc.,
919 Third Avenue, New York, New York 10022, U.S.A.

CONTENTS

INTRODUCTION

Are you one of the frightened? Does your story appear in this book? Pull up a chair and prepare yourself. Make sure the doors are bolted, the windows locked and the fireplace roaring with blazing logs. There must be no dark corners, no murky shadows, no questionable areas where no light falls.

You are about to go on a journey into the undiscovered realm of the grotesque. A land where a man cannot escape his fate, where a cat can terrify a human being, where a woman is capable of lifting her head off her shoulders to re-do her hair, where a curious man with a strange umbrella follows you down the street . . . and the great unknown of uncertainty is poised at every turn of the road.

Settle back while I darken the room a little bit more. Now let's see if you are one of the frightened.

Boris Karloff

The Man in the Raincoat

The story of Sylvester Dodge

Have you ever imagined somebody following you? Caught a glimpse of a strange face in the crowd behind you? Then that face seems mysteriously with you wherever you go? Sylvester Dodge had just such an experience. Walk with me a bit and I'll tell you about Sylvester and his man in the raincoat—

Sylvester Dodge was a man like you or me. He worked as a bookkeeper in a Wall Street office and for many years he was saving for the day when he could afford his trip to Europe away from ledgers and bank balances and adding machines. Finally, the last week of daily toil approached and anticipation thrilled his fat little body as he boarded the Lexington Avenue local. The big vacation loomed on his horizon as the reward of a dreary lifetime.

It was then that Sylvester Dodge first noticed the man in the raincoat with the curiously shaped umbrella. Something about the man made Sylvester shudder. The man's face was a deathly white and the hands surrounding the handle of the umbrella were like great claws. The flesh of the fingers was horribly gnarled and ghastly green. Sylvester could not bear to look at him. But even in turning away, he felt the eyes of the man boring into his back like twin beams of awful light. You know the feeling, don't you? Someone who's looking at you, staring at you, eyeing you with such a terrible concentration that you want to scream or cry out, "Stop! Stop!"

When the train reached the station, Sylvester rushed from the car like a man released from prison. The man in the subway had shocked him. But then again, you do meet all kinds of people in New York, don't you? And so Sylvester Dodge began the block walk to his office. The sun was out, April breezes caressed the stone buildings and people bustled along with spring steps. But Sylvester had that curious feeling I mentioned to you—someone was following him. He felt eyes peering at his back, could feel somebody's interest and attention focused on his rounded body hurtling through the crowd.

He found himself walking faster. He stopped for a streetlight, puffing for air—he turned—a deathly white face in the crowd bobbed like a Halloween skeleton and vanished. Sylvester Dodge whirled and raced across the street, his coatails flying. He stopped again, a block away from his office, and flung a backward look. There was the man in the raincoat, waving his clawlike hand in greeting, the umbrella dangling from the wrist. Something pounded in Sylvester Dodge's skull and desperately, he raced the remaining block and fell against the building wall gasping for breath. He turned slowly, fighting for his reason.

But no—there was the man with the raincoat, a scant ten yards away, coming toward him. The ghastly face was smiling and the umbrella was outstretched almost as if it were seeking something. Sylvester Dodge pushed out from the wall and left the protection of the building.

At that precise moment, the grand piano that was being hoisted to the office on the fourth floor swung awkwardly on its pulley—the rope snapped and its great weight crashed to the sidewalk, pinning Sylvester Dodge to his death. So you see, poor Sylvester tried to run away from his fate and dodged in the wrong direction. All because he had the silly notion that someone was following him . . . well, I'll leave you here, my friend. You don't think my face is so awfully white, do you? Oh, I'm sorry. I seem to have dropped my umbrella. Would you mind very much handing it to me . . . ?

The Deadly Dress

The story of Dolores Martinez

Do you believe a dead person's property becomes invested with the spirit of that person? Haven't you had the feeling sometimes that you were wearing another person's clothes—even though you've just brought them brand new in some shop?

Step into my store for a minute. I want to tell you about Dolores Martinez. And a dress that she wore to the big wedding on Rivington Street . . .

Dolores was about your size, my dear. Small and shapely with lovely features. She was only nineteen at the time of the wedding party to which she and all of the neighborhood had been invited. But Dolores was not happy. Her little brother Juan got into a gang fight on the way back from the cleaner's with Dolores' one and only party dress. It was ruined. Now Dolores was as kind and understanding as she was sweet. Yet when she saw the dress, she could not hold back the tears. The wonderful party—how could she hope to attend it now that her beautiful gown was in shreds?

But Momma Martinez was determined that her daughter would not suffer a disappointment. She would go to the party and be the best dressed young lady there! With all the zeal and effort of a loving mother, Momma Martinez gathered the last few dollars in the house, snatched up her shawl and hurried forth into the street. But it was late—and many stores were closed. But the old lady was dauntless. Soon her tireless feet led her to a dimly lit clothing store somewhere on the East Side. Momma Martinez rushed in.

There was a funny little man on the other side of the counter. He smiled at her in greeting but his face was yellow with age and a lone tooth in his mouth glinted with the light of the overhead bulb. Momma Martinez poured out her needs and the old man rubbed his hands.

"Ten dollars?" he cackled. "I have just the dress. A real steal." He brought out a lovely pink organdy dress folded gently over his arms. Yes, yes—a stitch here, a stitch there and it would be perfect for Dolores.

For hours, Dolores stood patiently while Momma Martinez' skilled old fingers wrought their magic on the dress. The party was only minutes away now, but at last Dolores stood attired ready for the party. Small, imperial and elegant. She would easily be the belle of the ball. The dress did feel a little tight but she was properly dressed now. She was going to her party—it was all that mattered!

And what a party it was. Every boy in the neighborhood wanted to dance with Dolores Martinez. And did. And she whirled about the room on the arm of one swain after another. She did suffer some discomfort from tightness of the dress but Momma's sewing was firm, and the dress held.

But the girl inside the dress slowly began to come apart. First, a feeling of being confined. Then somewhere in the middle of a lively polka, Dolores suddenly felt her throat constrict. Her hands were clammy and moist. She pushed away from her partner, her fingers flying to her face. And then—as the music and the dancing reached. a fever pitch—the lovely girl in the organdy dress pitched forward on her face.

She was dead before anyone could reach her. The dress? The old storekeeper had done a terrible thing. Selling a dress that some other poor girl had been buried in . . . Oh, there are explanations. The formaldehyde seeping into the dress from a dead body. The heat of the dancing . . . Dolores' poor circulation. But, what do you think? They say that clothes make the man. I rather think that clothes make the corpse . . . But come, step into my shop. I have a pretty pink dress just your size, my dear. Would you like to try it on?

The Hand of Fate

The story of Vashtu Singh

Have you ever tried to run away from something? You do everything in your power to put something off—defeat the hand of fate—then it happens anyway? You must know what I mean. Surely in your own lifetime you've tried to avoid someone or something only to have destiny come upon you as inexorably as the grave approaches us.

Draw your chair closer to the fire. No, no, no, don't you ever heard the incredible tale of Vashtu Singh? He was a Hindu manservant and what happened to him in India a long time ago is something no living soul can afford to ignore. So, listen closely . . .

Ugly vultures wheeled through the summer sky that day. And the people of the village bowed their heads toward Mecca. It was a time of the plague and starvation and the streets were filled with the wasted bodies of Death. Something hung like a pall in the air. Something poised to strike . . . but there was only prayer to comfort the sick . . .

The wants of the house had been many and the master had sent his trusted servant, Vashtu Singh, into the village to stock up on food and supplies for the oncoming week. The sands in the glass had shifted many times over and the master was impatient for the return of Vashtu Singh. But he was not prepared for the sight of his manservant rushing into the house, his turban awry, his eyes wild and unreasoning. A flurry of frightened words bubbled on Vashtu Singh's lips. The master quieted him down and asked to hear what had occurred.

"Master," pleaded Vashtu Singh, "I was in the market place to buy food. I saw Death. He looked right at me. Master—you must give me your fastest horse and I will ride to Samara to escape my fate."

The master listened, and knowing the ways of the Hindu, gave Vashtu the horse he needed and bade him flee at all possible speed. But after the servant had gone, the master's curiosity got the better of him. Garbing himself in a flowing burnoose, he went out to the stable, mounted a horse and rode into the village. The market place was teeming with life and hoarse cries of vendors urging sales to the passersby, but the master saw Death standing in the middle of the crowd. The master drew abreast of him and dismounted. Death saw him coming and waited, the blackness of his robes offset by the deadly wax of his features. But the master was not afraid of Death. He was angry at the loss of his favorite servant.

"See here," he demanded angrily. "What the devil do you mean by frightening my manservant like that? Now he's gone off and it's all your fault."

The utter surprise on the white face of Death was unmistakably genuine. "I am sorry," he said in a flat, sepulchral tone. "I myself was very startled to see

Vashtu Singh here in the market place. You see, I have an appointment with him tomorrow . . . *In Samarra*."

So you see how it is. Vashtu Singh, like so many of us, tried to run away from his destiny—only to run right into it. Feeling cold . . . ? Draw closer to the fire . . . There, isn't that better? And remember. Please don't be late for our appointment tomorrow. You know how I hate to wait . . . and I will catch up to you eventually.

Don't Lose Your Head

The story of Henry Harper

It must have happened to you some time in your life. You meet a completely strange set of people—they come into your life as suddenly as they leave—and they leave you to wonder the rest of your days. Was it real? Did you dream them all up? And why were you chosen, of all people, to encounter them? Here, have a glass of port while I tell you the strange story of Henry Harper, a traveling salesman . . .

It was in Shanghai, I think, shortly after the second World War, that Henry Harper had his curious experience. Now, Henry Harper was a rug salesman, which has little to do with the story. Except perhaps to explain that he was a man used to hotels, sleeping away from home, and who was constantly traveling in strange cities far away from his native London. So it was that Henry Harper found himself in an obscure Shanghai hotel, a guest for one night; in the morning he had an important appointment with one of the wealthiest dealers in the city.

Henry Harper was tired. The noisy, jostling Shanghai streets, a veritable melting pot of races, colors and creeds, had given him a headache. His eyeballs were scorched from the afternoon sun. So it was that when night came, Henry Harper was more than ready for bed. He had unpacked all his luggage, attired himself in pajamas, and read himself to sleep as had been his custom for many years. But he had fallen asleep with the lights on. It was perhaps an hour or two later that Henry Harper stirred restlessly in his bed. His eyes were still closed but a curious, *scratching* noise came to his ears. Shanghai's street noises had abated somewhat and now the scratching sound filled the tiny room. Henry Harper sat erect peevishly and opened his eyes to see what the disturbance was. He was hardly prepared for the sight that greeted him.

Seated at the dresser in the room, just at the foot of his bed, her back to him, was a lovely Eurasian woman, busily combing her hair, as nice as you please. The woman's hair was fantastically long; its black length trailing down her shoulders to the floor. Henry Harper could only gape as the comb in the lady's hand ran briskly through the beautiful hair with easy, feminine strokes. It was the noise of the comb drawing through the hair that had awakened Henry Harper.

Before he could open his mouth to speak to the lady, she had encountered some difficulty. The comb became snarled in a clump of her hair. Without a moment's hesitation, the lady *lifted her head off her shoulders* and disentangled the comb from her hair. Henry Harper had seen enough. With terror chilling his brain, he sprang out of bed and flung into the room next to his like a wild man.

Four bland Chinese men were seated about a deal table having a quiet game of cards. Henry screamed to them about the woman in his room who had removed her head before his very eyes. The four Chinese smiled up at Henry Harper.

"Oh, that," they said in chorus. "That's nothing. We can all do *that*." Whereupon, they all in turn *lifted their heads off their shoulders*.

So you see Henry Harper had quite an experience. Of course, no one at the sanitarium believes this, but there you are. I suppose people always expect traveling salesmen to have a lot of funny stories to tell . . . By the way, help yourself to a cigar while I step through the wall here and go down to the cellar for another bottle of port. I do hate to take the long way.

Call at Midnight

The story of John Le Grew

Do you have trouble sleeping at night? Do you find yourself tossing restlessly in bed? I wonder why? Perhaps you saw something during the waking day that troubled you. What was it—that strange man on the bus? Or the curious manner of that woman in the drug store? Or maybe your story is like the bizarre incident in the life of John Le Grew. Let me tell you about him . . .

John Le Grew was a bachelor. But not by choice. For twelve long years since the war he had supported his ailing mother and denied his own happiness. You see, his anemic salary at the watch factory had not permitted any thoughts of increasing the Le Grew household.

But John once had something out of life. During 1944 in France, he had met Denise Françon, the wonderful little French girl who had been the only love of John's shallow life. But a bombardment of her little village and the silence that followed had left John with only one conclusion. Denise was dead. Well, the war ended and he had returned to America and his mother. And the watch factory. And the dull years had ticked away with the clocks.

But one day everything changed. John came home

after a day at the factory and his mother said a girl named Denise had called and wanted to talk to him. John couldn't believe his ears. There was some mistake. Denise was dead—she had to be—but no. During dinner the telephone in the hallway rang again. John rushed to answer it. It was impossible, it was unbelievable. But the sweet voice on the other end of the line was the same broken English of Denise Françon.

And a dozen questions spilled from his heart. Where was she? How had she been? Why had she waited all these years to get in touch with him? Did she still love him? But oddly, Denise couldn't say much. Her voice seemed faint and shaky. But she gave a telephone number—Butterfield 8-7777—and insisted that John call her at that number at twelve midnight.

All the rest of the evening John was in a fever of impatience. The tiny clock on the bureau mocked him as the hour and minute hands slowly crawled around to the appointed hour. Finally, it was midnight, and John lifted the phone from the hook and dialed the number. A male voice asked who was calling. Surprised, John wanted to know if he had the right number. Yes, it was Butterfield 8-7777. Who did he want to speak to? John asked for Denise Françon.

The voice, replied, "I don't seem to recognize the name."

John's voice trembled. "I'm sorry," he said. "But this number was given to me to call at midnight and—"

The man's voice interrupted him, saying, "Of course. Denise Françon? Yes, certainly, I remember now. The body was delivered for embalming yesterday morning—looks like an automobile accident—and yet—"

Oh well, in the midst of life we are in death. John Le Grew hung up and sat in his chair staring at the wall for a long, long time . . . and to this day he still sits staring at a wall and hears a voice. A soft-sweet trembling voice asking him to call and call and call . . . Well, I leave you. This is Woodlawn. Oh, I thought you knew. The Woodlawn Cemetery is my destination. You see, I live here . . . Goodbye . . . for a while . . . and do call me when you get a chance . . .

Just Inside the Cemetery

The story of Arthur Wingate

Arthur Wingate was a fairly well-to-do lawyer in the small town of Morrisville. It's a quiet, orderly town. Nothing out of the way ever happens there. Or so he thought for thirty years. But then one day all of it changed—and his whole life lay before him. Like the day he saw those men digging that fresh grave just inside the cemetery gate on his way home from work. You resemble Arthur Wingate, friend. Listen closely and you may avoid the terrible thing that happened to him . . .

It had been a hot, dusty day in Morrisville. Possibly it was the hot sun, but a sudden headache came over Arthur Wingate. His hands were moist, his brow feverish. He decided to go home to his own farm land just over the hill beyond the town. It wasn't too long a walk and maybe the fresh air would do him some good. So Arthur Wingate left his office and walked slowly down Main Street. It was odd but he met no one on the way. Soon, he was drawing abreast of the long, low-lying wall that bordered Morrisville's only cemetery. The rhythmic sound of pickaxes attacking the soft sod came to him from beyond the wall. Someone had died. Life and Death went on in Morrisville same as any other town. But opposite the front gate where the sounds of digging were loudest, Arthur Wingate suddenly halted in confusion. No one had died recently to his knowledge except the Starkey boy and his burial had been a month ago.

Puzzled, Arthur Wingate went into the cemetery, and, just inside the wall, two men were grimly spading the earth into heaping ugly mounds. The heads and shoulders of the men were barely visible. Arthur Wingate approached them both and asked them what they were doing. The faces of the two men were strange to him but they both seemed to consider his question even stranger.

"Somebody died," the taller of the two sneered and they both jeered at Arthur Wingate, whose headache was suddenly worse. Feverishly, he stumbled from the cemetery and finally reached home. The day had been too much for him. He fell into a long exhausted sleep. But his mind would not let him rest. The scene at the cemetery stayed with him. Who could have died?

Arthur Wingate felt the cold wind of something fan his spine. He had a curious sensation of unreality that he could not shake off. He could not wait a second longer. He left his home near midnight and ran to the cemetery. It looked eerie, forlorn and cold in the midnight. The metal gate squealed as he stepped inside. He splashed light in the direction of where he remembered the grave to be. It was still there—but there was something else too.

A pine box was placed to one side of the grave, its lid angled backward to show the contents. Arthur Wingate drew nearer and slowly, fearfully, aimed his flashlight at the interior of the oblong box. The fact that it was empty was far more frightening than if it had been occupied. There was a tag on the box, dangling from a metal hinge. The wind in the graveyard howled and tore at the thing as Arthur Wingate held it up to the light.

Scrawled across the tab in a spidery hand were the words . . . ARTHUR WINGATE . . .1907—1964. He saw no more. A hideous scream ripped from his throat and he pitched forward into the empty box, the lid slamming down behind him, shutting him in.

Of course, when they found him there the next morning he was dead. Heart attack. Nothing had been written on the tag except a series of numbers indicating the grave's dimensions. And the box had been for the Starkey boy because his grave was being moved at his mother's request. But Arthur Wingate had met his death . . . by premonition, by fate, by manifest destiny . . .

Yes, perhaps it's an interesting tale . . . quiet, unusual . . . but I hear them all the time . . . in my business, you understand . . . huh? Oh, I'm an undertaker . . . can I interest you in a plot of ground . . . at our summer rates?

The Fortuneteller

The story of the Gamboli triplets

Have you had your fortune told recently? Did the gypsy read cards or look into a crystal ball to tell you what the future holds in store for you? The three Gamboli sisters wanted to know. And their fortuneteller told them one sunny day in Italy. Now, the Gamboli sisters were triplets. They were as alike as three peas in a pod and their names were Rita, Gessa and Lena. In the little village of Lombardi, their fame and beauty was widespread. And since their parents' death, they had supported themselves as seamstresses.

Their nineteenth birthday was the day of the big festival in the town square, and the sisters went into the tent of the fortuneteller and demanded of the old crone there to know their fortunes and how soon they would marry. The old crone gazed into the crystal and shook her craggy, ancient head.

"You will never marry, my dears," she cackled. "Because you'll all be dead before the year is out." The girls laughed, but deep in their hearts there was a dim sense of fear. The bony fingers singled out Rita. She would die of pneumonia. Gessa and Lena trembled when the old woman whispered something far more terrible about them. Gessa would die at Lena's hand and Lena in turn would die because of her sister's death. Now they were sure the old woman was crazy, and shouting insults at her, they bounced out of the tent to seek their admirers and the warmth and gaiety of the festival. But the old gypsy's words stayed with them.

Within a month, Rita died on the night of a full moon. Of pneumonia. Gessa and Lena were heartbroken and chilled with the prophecy that seemed to be coming true. All the village mourned and the girls in their bereavement sought to find some comfort in love. But such is fortune, they both fell in love with the same man. A tall, dashing man of the village, Antonio.

Lena and Gessa had always loved each other as sisters but now they were women both vying for the same man. One night, three months to the day of Rita's death, they went at each other like tigresses in their little hut on the north end of the village. In a craze of passion, Lena plunged her seamstress shears deep into Gessa's heart. Lena, overcome first with remorse and then fear, dragged her sister's body out to the well and with the strength of the guilty one who hides a crime, dropped Gessa's body down into the dark, slimy interior. She fled back into the house and fell on her knees before the statue of the Madonna on the kitchen wall and prayed for forgiveness. In her mad desire for Antonio, she had forgotten the gypsy woman's dire prophecy.

Now she had Antonio. And she told the people of the village that Gessa had run away because Antonio preferred her—her sister. But on the day of the wedding, Lena, resplendent in her bridal gown, went to the well and stared down into the place where her sister's body was hidden from the eyes of the world. In the few inches of dirty, slimey water at the well's bottom, she saw the huddled outline of Gessa's decayed body there. Quite unexpectedly, a bat flew up out of the well and settled in Lena's black, luxuriant hair. Screaming and twisting, she tried to beat it off, but the bat flapped its wings maddeningly and hung on. Lena whirled and tripped over the rim of the well, screaming like a banshee, her fingernails raking the walls as she fell.

When the townspeople lowered a ladder into the well, they found the bodies. And even Antonio could see that the point of the seamstress shears sticking out through Gessa's back had knifed right into Lena's falling body. So the prophecy was filled . . . Rita died of pneumonia, Lena killed Gessa and Gessa killed Lena . . . a triplet slay you might call it . . . but where was I? . . . oh yes . . . I think you're going to kill somebody . . .

The Vampire Sleeps

The story of Count Alexis

Do you whistle past the graveyard? Perhaps you are really so like the rest of us. Come with me—just a short ride through the hills past the old burial grounds where Count Alexis met the lady in the long, flowing veil . . .

The famous castle of the Alexis family had long towered in the hillside in the Bavarian valley. Count Alexis, himself the last surviving member of the historic brood, was tall and handsome and kind. Indeed, the only wonder in the village was when he would marry and raise a son to continue the glory of his ancestors.

And then one storm-tossed night when he was out on the marshes with his hunting dog, Alexis saw a tall, beautiful dark-haired woman in a long, flowing veil, walking across the meadows toward him. It seemed her carriage had overturned on the bridge and crashed into the raging waters of the Kasne River. Her driver and horses had perished but she had managed to save herself. The Count had already surrendered to the romance of their meeting. Only the hound dog seemed to whimper and growl and behave badly whenever the lady drew near him. But the Count insisted that the lady be his guest and took her straight to his castle.

Within a fortnight, Alexis had wooed and won her

and all the village celebrated the wonderful news. Alexis
would have an heir. But in the days preceding the marriage, the young Count seemed to be failing in health.
He lost weight so that his uniforms seemed to hang on
him, and curiously enough, to the staff of the castle,
Sonia, their future mistress, fairly glowed with health
since her ordeal in the river.

But when no one could recall seeing her in the day-
time, rumors began to spread. The old wives' tales
about vampires who stalk at night and sleep in the day-
time swept through the village like wildfire. And finally
up in the master bedroom where he lay exhausted,
Count Alexis himself had to credit the rumors. How else
this sudden loss of weight and failing health? And why
should Sonia's blooming good health coincide exactly
with the loss of his own vitality? Count Alexis made up
up his mind. He pulled the bell cord by his bed and
summoned his manservant. When the fellow appeared,
the Count asked that his fiancee be brought to him!
But the servant shook his head—the Lady Sonia had
gone out before dawn, riding off to the west as was her
usual custom.

Count Alexis had heard enough. He dressed, armed
himself with a short dagger and ordered his fastest
horse. He thundered down the castle road off to the
west, toward the very spot where he had first met Sonia.
The meadows were barren and darkness was coming on.
The Count led his horse carefully over the hilly ground.
Finally, he found what he was looking for. A stone slab
set in the earth covered over with vines and leaves.
Triumphantly he dragged it to one side, and looking
down, he could just make out an open coffin with Sonia

lying in it, her pale beauty and blood red lips gleaming in the dying light.

Alexis drew his dagger and raised it for the kill. It is said the only way you can kill a vampire . . . a stake through the heart while it sleeps. But suddenly, the dagger fell from his fingers and a slow, eerie smile played over his face. Like a stone man, he settled down beside her. To wait for the vampire's hour. For he had learned Sonia's secret too late. Too late to stop him from becoming a vampire himself . . .

See now, my friend? Those two bats wheeling through the darkness? It is Sonia and Count Alexis winging through the night waiting for the chance to assume human form again . . . you don't believe me? . . . I'm sorry . . . the people of the village will believe nothing else. My, but you do have a soft delicate throat . . .

Mirror of Death

The story of Celeste Collins

Did you ever break a mirror and spend the rest of the day in dread—wondering what awful fate would befall you? It *is* bad luck to break a mirror, you know. Because the gods in the mirror are protecting you from harm. And when you break your particular mirror, you are darkening the vision of your protectors and anything is liable to happen.

Take the strange tale of Celeste Collins. She was a pretty Irish girl and on the day of her twenty-first birthday the girls in the office were giving her a luncheon party. She was dressing in her bedroom, arranging her hair in a stunning coiffure and admiring herself in her hand mirror. Her hair was her crowning glory, the envy of the girls at the office. And so she preened herself in the mirror, first turning this way and that, completely satisfied with the effect. But she set the mirror down carelessly, and it slipped off the dresser, falling to the floor with a shattering sound of broken glass. Celeste wrinkled her pretty nose and shrugged. Just another mirror. At any rate, it was time to go to work.

She hurried from the house to catch the subway. While she was fumbling in her purse for a token, it splayed open and all the contents spilled out under the turnstile. Reaching under the stile to put her bag together only caused a long run in each of her nylon stockings. Then she was an hour late for work because the train stalled in the tunnel and tied up transportation, and at the office, she overturned a bottle of ink on the whole pile of contracts she had typed so carefully the day before. Well, by noon, Celeste had decided that it was just one of those days when you should have stayed in bed.

Although Celeste Collins was Irish and the Irish are fey—steeped in the traditions of leprechauns and strange happenings—she was practical and sensible as well as pretty. The broken mirror was just a coincidence and just a silly superstition anyway. The birthday party that followed erased any doubts she may have had in mind. The girls wined her and dined her in the little restaurant around the corner. They had even gotten her a birthday cake. Even though the morning had been awful, the rest of the day flew by with Celeste as happy as a bird.

And so, at five o'clock, she went home. Her birthday had been a great success. It was only an hour later while she was sewing a dress in the living room that the doorbell rang. Expectantly, Celeste sprang to answer. It was a delivery man, with a large upright package that towered as high as the door. Celeste signed for it as the man moved the package to the center of the room and propped it up against the table. After he had left, she eyed the heavy cords that bound the package and suddenly realized that the girls had taken this method of surprising her with a birthday present. Delightedly, she took her sewing shears and cut the cords. The wrapping paper fell away with a hissing noise and miraculously there were two Celeste Collins in the room. The one standing away from the table, the other smiling back from the reflected depths of the full-length mirror propped against the table.

But Celeste Collins started to scream. The face in the mirror was a twisted, satanic thing. An outrageous duplication of the lovely face before it. Celeste stepped back, overwhelmed with fright. She kept backing up but the awful thing in the mirror receded with her And then her legs were halted by the sill of the window behind her. Whirling, Celeste saw her face again in the crystal-clear panes of glass in the windows. The same hideous ghastly smile. With a terrible shriek, she hurled herself at the window and fell through. Six stories to the cement courtyard below . . .

So you see, my friend, the birthday present was a gift from Hell. Of course Celeste saw only herself in the mirror. But look for yourself. Look into the mirror . . . oh, do be careful . . . there . . . you've dropped it . . . broken it into a million fragments . . . how dreadful . . . I'm afraid you're in for some bad luck . . .

Never Kick a Black Cat

The story of Felix Darnell

Do you see that black cat just ahead of you? Look out! It may cross your path with a sudden dart of its black, furry body. Now, you know that old superstition about not letting a black cat walk across your path—do you believe it? If you do—or even if you don't—perhaps you'll be interested in hearing the strange tale of Felix Darnell and the cat that screamed in the night, high above the streets of the city . . .

It was a cold, dreary, rain-swept day when Felix Darnell first met the cat. Felix Darnell was a construction foreman on the Welles-Spencer project on the lower East Side. The Welles-Spencer building was already thirteen stories high and, with but seven more floors to go, the building would be one of the mightiest and most ultra-modern structures on the East Side.

Felix Darnell was a tall, thin scarecrow of a man but the muscles of his body were taut and finely strung through his deceiving frame. He was foreman of an older day—indeed he might have worked on the pyramids or the colossus of Rhodes. But Felix Darnell was a lonely man with no one to share his pride. He ate alone and lived alone and walked alone. And on this cold and dreary rain-swept day, he walked to his job, staring down at the sidewalk. Suddenly on the pavement before him, a long, thin black cat stalked from an alley and halted on its haunches. Felix Darnell did not see the cat until he nearly stumbled across it.

Felix Darnell snapped out of his reverie and cursed. Cats! He hated cats. He aimed a vicious kick at it. The cat howled in pain and slunk off, miserable and wet in the rain. Felix reached the project, changed into his overalls and cap and took the lift to the thirteenth floor. Now, the rain had abated somewhat but looking at the scaffolds and catwalks, Felix Darnell was not happy. It would slow up the job. He cursed again.

Suddenly, Felix Darnell heard a crying, moaning noise. A low fierce sound like someone in agony. Could someone be stuck out on the framework, trapped on one of the catwalks? Taking a flashlight because the day was dark and unnaturally still, he stepped out on the catwalk that ran on a straight line to what would be a southwest corner of the building. He walked slowly and carefully along the thin iron ledge that held his weight. The street yawned beneath him—thirteen construction floors down. And then a dark figure, balled and indescribable, sprang from a dim niche and shot toward Felix Darnell. He had one awful second to see the two eyes burning in the cat's head.

The same cat he had kicked only an hour before. The feline body raced between his legs on the catwalk. With a horrible scream, he tried to balance himself, fought for survival. His hands clawed at the air but his weight had been thrown to one side by the cat's movement. He hung into space for a brief instant before he fell. All the way to the street—thirteen floors below. He landed on a steel beam waiting to be hauled up and what it did to him was something that would make even a cat turn away in disgust . . .

Interesting tale of revenge, isn't it? Felix Darnell and his black cat . . . of course, it might be just a coincidence, but . . . there . . . look . . . we can find out for ourselves . . . a black cat just crossed your path . . . see him go? . . . do you mind if I stay with you, my friend? . . . I'd like to see for myself just what happens to you . . .

The Ladder

The story of Gaspard and Francois

Careful now—do not by any means walk under the ladder that someone has placed so carelessly against the building wall there. Possibly a sign painter is working there—but that ladder can only bring you trouble. Did you ever hear the tale of the two robbers? It was in the days of medieval history. The days of darkness and gothic gloom . . . and death . . .

Their names were Gaspard and Francois. They were young men but old in the ways of treachery and villainy. They had cut throats for fun as well as for money. Gaspard and Francois lived by their wits and the quickness of their fingers and daggers. But one April night, Gaspard and Francois rousted and reveled in the infamous tavern of Le Coq d'Or. They had been idle for days and so had taken recourse in drunken debauchery. Their fingers itched for their curious profession, they hungered to play their wicked trade.

And so when a fat wealthy merchant left the tavern after announcing loudly to one and all of his riches in his little house at the end of town, Gaspard and Francois lurched in pursuit. The Paris streets were dark and ill-lit but the two drunken thieves followed their prey with eyes long used to the darkness. Happily, the distance was not far. Soon the fat merchant turned into a cobbled courtyard and entered an ivy-covered stone building. Gaspard and Francois waited patiently and when candlelight flickered in a second story window, they made their plans.

It was the work of only a moment to climb the wall surrounding the house. In the darkness of the courtyard, they found a crude wooden ladder propped near the barn door. Gaspard placed it gently against the vines until the top rung rested directly below the fat merchant's window. Francois licked his lips greedily and his dirty fingers tightened about the dagger in his hand. He would make short work of the fat merchant. But Gaspard was already mounting the ladder as stealthily as a cat; his knife gleaming in the darkness.

He had very nearly reached the top rung when the casement windows flew open and there was the fat merchant thrusting a lighted torch into his face. Gaspard screamed terribly, lashing out with his knife but this fat merchant had been rich too long and stayed fat because he had known how to take care of himself and his money. The long sword in his fat fingers buried itself in Gaspard's chest up to the hilt. At the bottom of the ladder, Francois panicked and scrambled off the rungs, coming around behind the ladder and hiding underneath it, hugging the wall. He stared up above him as the great bulk of Gaspard's dead body sagged against the rungs. The merchant was shouting for the police at the top of his lungs. Francois was frozen where he stood, the drunkenness of the evening still boiling in his blood. His eyes flashed about the courtyard looking for the best avenue of escape.

And then—Gaspard's body, unevenly fixed on the

ladder, toppled through the space of one set of rungs and landed heavily on his partner Francois. Francois' eyes bulged with surprise and a bloody moan bubbled from his dirty throat as the point of the sword jutting from Gaspard's back knifed into his heart. When the police arrived to see what the commotion was, they found Gaspard and Francois huddled behind the ladder, jammed against the wall. Like two frightened children locked in each other's arms against the cold—and there you are.

Legend has it, of course, that Francois walked under a ladder and died terribly. But . . . well, you've heard the story and—so please be careful . . . you never can tell, can you? Well, upon my soul . . . here comes the sign painter to get his ladder—and do you know, my friend, you've been standing under it for the longest time . . . ?

Nightmare!

The story of John Day

Did you ever feel as if you couldn't breathe? Your tongue is thick in your mouth—your throat is hoarse—your lungs are bursting for air. It seems as if the walls of your room are closing in on you. Crushing you, crowding you, sealing you off from the rest of the world. And then you awake. It's only been a ghastly dream. A terribly vivid nightmare. But with your eyes open and your hands trembling and your body bathed in perspiration—you relax. At least you are in your own room. Safe. And it was only a dream. Or was it . . . ?

This is a tale that the inmates of Bell Prison still whisper to this day in the cell yards and corridors. The story of John Day, a lifer, and his weird nocturnal dreams. It happened long ago but Cell 13, where it began, still enjoys its haunted history. Listen and I'll tell you about John Day and his nightmares . . .

One night at twelve midnight, the stone and steel corridors of Row A rang with the hoarse, terrible shouts of a man screaming for the guards. The prisoners so rudely awakened would normally have grumbled and yelled their annoyance but something in the horrible moans and sobbings issuing from Cell 13 stilled their tongues. The guards rushed to the cell and swung it open to find John Day crouched in the corner on the

floor by his bed, now whimpering and crying, his hands
to his throat. At the sight of the guards, he blurted
about his nightmare.

". . . the hands," he babbled, "the hands. Thick, calloused, lumpy hands. They were choking me . . ."

Just a nightmare, the guards laughed. But that wasn't
the end of it. It was only the beginning of many nights
when Row A would be similarly disturbed. John Day
and his nightmare about someone strangling him became the talk of Bell Prison. And John Day himself,
sentenced to life imprisonment, grew steadily thinner
and paler. The warden refused to listen to his pleas for
another cell. He wouldn't cater to the whims of con-
victs. The prison doctor insisted that John Day was only
shamming because other than a loss of weight, he was
organically and mentally sound.

But still the nightmare persisted and John Day's nocturnal outcries became a familiar sound that the prisoners accepted as another rigor of their hard existence.
But one night came a new sound. The escape sirens
wailed over the yard—John Day had escaped. Attacked
a guard and gone over the wall. The entire organization
of Bell Prison went into action. Guards with blood-
hounds scoured the surrounding countryside. And only
two miles away, one guard with his dog came on a
strange sight. A teamster with his heavy wagon pulled
over to one side of the road. And lying on the ground,
still in his prison uniform, his eyes bulging unnaturally
in his head, lay John Day. He was dead.

The guard approached the big teamster, a burly
giant, and questioned him. The story was simple
enough. John Day had halted him with a gun to make

use of the wagon and the teamster had fought back. Luckily, John Day's gun had misfired and the man had been able to get his hands around his throat. The guard shone his flashlight on the teamster's hands. They were thick, calloused and lumpy . . . big thorny fingers that had strangled the life out of John Day . . .

Only a nightmare, Bell Prison had thought . . . just a convict's curious dream . . . but when John Day's dead body was returned to the prison morgue, the story of Cell 13 became the terrible tale it is to this day. And what of your dreams and your nightmares? If you ever imagine that fingers are at your throat, throttling you, don't twist and turn. Wake up. Open your eyes . . . maybe it is just a dream . . . but someone could be killing you . . .

Voice from the Grave

The story of Martin Cable

Surely you must have read "Hamlet" at some time or other in your life. If you did, do you recall that line—"There are more things in Heaven and Hell, Horatio, than are dreamt of in your philosophy"? Well, the strange tale that I am about to tell you is something like that. My story has to do with traveling and automobiles and a little girl. Do you believe that the dead can influence the living? But come—listen to the incredible history of Martin Cable and the little girl in the polka dot dress . . .

The road was dark and winding that grim night that Martin Cable drove his sedan toward Webb Center. Rain slashed, howled and tore at the windows. And Martin Cable was worried. His headlights had fused out and driving in unfamiliar territory down an unknown road on such a dreadful night was not the safest thing in the world. But Martin Cable was due in Webb Center for an important business meeting that could mean a new life for him. And so, he drove on, taking his chances . . . with the weather, with the car . . . with his life. Suddenly, through the windshield wipers mopping furiously at the glass, Martin Cable saw a flash of something up ahead. A white face in the darkness.

Hurriedly, he slammed on the brakes and the car

swerved to a halt. Martin Cable peered out on the road.
There was a little girl standing there, in a polka dress,
the rain pelting at her viciously, making a tangled mess
of her hair. The child's face was chalk white and ghostly.
Before Martin Cable could ask her anything she came
forward and put one tiny hand on the car window and
pointed down the road.

"Mister." Her small voice was pitiful. "You better
turn left here. There's a big hole in the ground just
ahead. You can't go that way." Gratefully, Martin
Cable thanked her and asked if he could give her a lift
home. She shook her head and indicated a grey cottage
just to the right of the road.

"I'll be all right," she said. "I live just there." So
Martin Cable took the turnoff and arrived safely at his
destination, tired and shaken but thankful that the little
girl had save his life. The next day when he inquired
about the road, the hotel clerk told him that a rock slide
had made an immense pit on the road that could kill
anyone who fell into it.

Well, Martin Cable completed his business in Webb
Center, paid a visit to a toy store and drove back the
way he had come. He had decided to reward the little
girl for her kindness of the night before. When he drew
his car up to the grey cottage, a peaceful serenity hung
over the walls and the windows. Martin Cable, with his
gift under his arm, knocked loudly on the little oaken
door. A small grey-haired woman came to see who it
was. Martin Cable introduced himself and explained his
visit. He wanted to see the little girl, he said.

"What little girl?" the woman asked. Martin Cable
rushed on to tell about the rain and being lost and saved

from certain death. "Describe her to me—" the lady said. "What was she wearing?" Confused, Martin Cable mentioned the polka dot dress. But he didn't understand until the lady shook her head sadly.

"Yes," she said. "It was Madeline. Once a year she comes to that part of the road and warns some traveler away from the very spot. It's been like that for five years now." But Martin Cable was dumfounded. What did the woman mean? Yet, it was all very simple. "Madeline was my daughter, and five years ago she died in an accident at the place where she told you to turn. You see, she got run over by a car there . . ."

Curious, isn't it? A little girl returning like that to warn the unwary traveler away from death. Oh, yes, if you're driving tonight—do be careful—there might be a nasty break in the road.

Theda Is Death

The story of Carlos Luga

There are moments in the magnified futility of our dreams when our best efforts are vastly and poignantly inadequate. We poise to leap from great ledges; towering mountains bow to our frantic feet while the gigantic demons bay at our heels. Escape lies below in the boiling waters of a bottomless ocean. But our feet are anchored in the mud beneath us. Escape . . . can we ever really escape the nightmare horror that reaches out for us? Carlos Luga tried. Even as you and I. But you can't run away from yourself, can you?

Carlos Luga was a steward on the freighter *Caledonia* just after the last war. The *Caledonia* was a familiar sight churning through the quiet waters of the Caribbean and Carlos Luga, a young Mexican boy of twenty-two, was happy with his job. That is until he met the tall, dark man in the cloak on the midnight watch. The Caribbean moon was huge that wondrous, still night but Carlos Luga felt cold and afraid. The tall, dark man approached him and asked for a light for his cigarette. And while thumbing a lighter for the gentleman, Carlos suddenly realized that he could remember no passenger who answered this description. The man walked on without Carlos seeing his face. And somehow the deck, shifting with the moving sea, was funereal and unreal.

And so it went—night after night during the watch, the cloaked man would stroll past Carlos Luga, quietly, on gliding feet, and cold chills would spread over the boy's spine. At the end of the voyage, Carlos Luga was afraid. He crossed himself many times but he demanded of the owners of the line to be transferred to another ship. The boy was so earnest and so obviously upset that his wishes were heeded.

Carlos was delegated to another ship—the passenger boat *Theda*. Standing on his first watch in the middle of the Caribbean, Carlos was happy for the first time in weeks. He felt as if some terrible weight had been lifted from his brown shoulders. And then a quiet voice at his elbow asked for a match. Carlos Luga trembled. He knew that terrible deadly voice. He turned, his tongue stuck in his throat, his heart hammering like the drums of the natives.

Standing before him was the tall, dark man. Carlos Luga could see the all-enveloping cloak, the slouch hat. But the face was in darkness. And Carlos Luga had seen all the passengers mounting the morning gangplank. But there had been no tall dark man. Carlos Luga controlled his trembling body with a great effort. An enormous terror welled within him but he reached for his lighter, struck it and thrust it into the face of his strange accoster. The bursting flame held for a second and Carlos Luga screamed. The face under the brim of the hat was his own! A hideous, deathly, skull-like caricature of his own.

The lighter fell from his numbed fingers and the tall, dark man before him laughed. A high-pitched, awful giggle. The laugh seemed to do something to Carlos

Luga. Still screaming, he pitched forward, his strong brown hands closing around the throat of the man before him. They locked together in a fantastic death dance on the rolling deck; the seas about the ship seeming to leap and beat to the struggle like an audience taking sides. The big moon overhead gleamed down mercilessly.

They found Carlos Luga the next morning . . . lying on his back . . . his own hands fastened to his own throat . . . his eyeballs bulging like ugly things . . . it was inconceivable . . . but the ship's doctor called it death by manual strangulation . . . *self-inflicted*. Curious tale, is it not?

But improbable as it might seem these things *do* happen . . . like the name of the ship where Carlos Luga met his terrible fate . . . the *Theda* . . . rearrange the letters . . . it's merely another anagram on the word *Death* . . . death spelled yet another way. You might say that *Theda* is *Death* spelled backward. Now, didn't Carlos Luga die . . . backward . . . ?

The Barking Dog

The story of Pedro and Tony

It is midnight. The minute and hour hands have joined, and one half of the world lies sleeping. It is daylight in China—and darkness in New York. But in some corners of the world it is always dark. There are dark corners which will never know light. Like the Black Hole of Calcutta, like the River Styx—or even the abandoned mine shaft in Loma Point, New Mexico. Where nobody could remember a night so dark.

The barking dog started it all. Pedro and Tony heard the dog, and being small, healthy boys of ten, paid heed. They were playing outside the old abandoned mine at Loma Point and they should have known better. Hadn't their mothers warned them so many times not to go in there? The mine was dangerous—the walls might cave in—the darkness was a den of so many wicked, terrible animals waiting to eat little boys alive! Pedro and Tony knew all this and with the sun going down should have been on their way home. But the dog kept barking. Loud, yipping yells—and boys are boys and dogs are dogs.

And Tony, poor little Tony; to his childish ears, it was the bark of Chiti, the spaniel who had disappeared from his world only a year ago. How could they *not* go into the tunnel that led to the mine shaft? Eagerly, adventurously, the boys darted into the gloomy interior. Still, the dog barked. They could hear his yelping somewhere in the distance, farther on. They disturbed a bat who suddenly wheeled over their heads, wings flapping furiously. And then a mammoth roar filled the tunnel—the ceiling behind them split and tons of rock and stone thundered down, sealing the entrance.

Frightened, the boys threw their arms about each other and shivered in the darkness. The air grew thick and heavy. Pedro began to cry but Tony dug out some cheap wooden matches. And still the dog barked—urgently, continuously. From some distant point ahead. Frantically, Tony pushed on, dragging the weeping Pedro with him—the pitifully short life of each match throwing ghastly, terrible shadows on the walls around them. And the dog barked and barked endlessly.

It's Chiti, thought Tony, hope pounding in his little chest—Chiti's calling to us! He's alive and helping us find a way out of the darkness . . .

The boys stumbled on, falling over rocks and wreckage in their way. And then suddenly, up ahead, so far away it looked like a star, a narrow crevice spilled open and moonlight trickled and gleamed. The boys flung toward it, gasping, still hearing the barking of a little dog. When they fell out of the small opening, they could see the mob of townspeople with torches, scouring the countryside for them. Small wonder. They'd been lost in the mine shaft for hours and their frightened mothers had been quick to act. Everyone was glad to find them safe and sound.

But you know how grownups are. Nobody, but nobody believed the story of the barking dog. Children's fancies and imaginations, they said . . . but Pedro and Tony know, as they know nothing else, that it was the barking of Chiti, faithful Chiti, that led them out of the awful darkness of the abandoned mine shaft at Loma Point. There now . . . do you hear it? That barking in the wilderness . . . that mournful howling . . . it's Chiti again . . . hear him? . . he's starting all over again . . .

Defilers of the Tombs

The story of Jonathan Jenkins

Laugh if you will but this is not a tale of humor. Jenkins once thought it so. He does not now. Jenkins was like you—like so many of us—laughing off the ghostly, turning his back on superstitions—refusing to accept the voices that scream in the night. Listen closely. You don't want to end up like Jonathan Jenkins, do you . . . ?

Jonathan Jenkins was an archeologist whose main fascination in life was Egypt. The land of the pharaohs and the Sphinx captured his imagination as no other ancient civilization ever had. So it was that when Jonathan Jenkins was delegated to lead an archeological expedition into the vast sands surrounding the Nile, he poured himself into the task with a fervor that belied his sixty years. The historical societies of the world were not surprised when three short months later, the Jenkins expedition reported the greatest find since the opening of King Tut's tomb.

Egyptology would take a giant step forward. Jenkins had uncovered what seemed to be a buried monument, tremendous in size, housing some of Egypt's oldest secrets. And then the world waited for more news— and terrible tales began to trickle out from the desert. The expedition had unearthed a stone door buried beneath the sands. The door had curious carvings and hieroglyphics. Jenkins' translation had been scholarly and precise: *"Defilers of the tombs of Egyptian kings, sleep no more."* It was the sort of warning archeologists are accustomed to. But strange events began to pile up at an alarming rate.

A junior member of the expedition suffocated to death when cut off from the rest of the party on a tour through the vaults. He had been trapped when a stone wall dropped behind him, sealing him off from help. Jenkins' colleague, Professor Artelli, died of scorpion poisoning when he picked up a curiously shaped scarab ring from its place in a tray of such objects. A hidden needle sprang out from a groove in the ring head when the professor's hand exerted pressure on it. Jenkins' wife, Theo, ran screaming from her tent one moon-crossed night, shouting that she had seen a man who "looked like a pharaoh" walking around her bed.

Common sense and civilized thinking did not help. All the deaths were explainable. The precautions the ancient Egyptians had taken against grave robbers had worked in the case of Professor Artelli and the junior member. But Jonathan Jenkins' wife was stark, raving mad in a period of three days. The "walking pharaoh" vision had stayed with her. And now the camp was an awful place to be. One by one, the native guides stole off into the night, running away. Never to return. And Jonathan Jenkins began to drink. Drink heavily. The Egyptian sun and the curse were working.

Soon, the camp was deserted except for Jenkins, his wife, and the lonesome moaning of a jackal in the night. But the scholarly Jenkins stumbled into his tent to record for posterity the terrible story of the expedition. He reached for foolscap and pen. The lantern swung off the table suddenly and the wind howled. And standing in the tent opening was a tall, erect figure. Jenkins recognized the face instantly. It was the same graven image of the designs etched on the sarcophagus deep in the crypt below the hill. The figure beckoned with one imperious finger. And Jenkins followed. Stumbling, falling—until he had reached the underground level of the inner, main tomb. The vault that housed the gigantic mummy case set on a dais in the center of the room . . . and then came the darkness and the awful chanting of voices long dead . . .

After weeks of no word from the Jenkins expedition, an investigating party arrived at the camp. The tents were deserted. Down in the valley, wandering among the silent stone edifices thrusting out of the sand, they found Theo Jenkins babbling insanely, completely out of her mind. Pressing on into the main tomb, they found Jonathan Jenkins—lying in the great mummy case, arms folded across his chest, cerements wrapped about him in the ancient Egyptian way. He had been dead for days. And no trace has been found, to this day, of the mummy that once must have occupied that sarcophagus . . . unless, of course, you choose to believe that the mummy case was *never* occupied in the first place . . . but come, why laugh at Egyptian curses? Unless you prefer to . . . sleep no more . . .

Terror in the Window

The story of Barton Frisbee

Someone who tells a strange tale is prone to regale a listener with just about anything that sounds impressive. It's human nature to say two when you mean only one—it's more interesting to kill ten people when there was, in reality, only one corpse. The terrible tale of Barton Frisbee is quite like that. With one startling difference. It is true . . . and it happened only last year.

Barton Frisbee was a window designer in one of the largest fashion shops in downtown Los Angeles. His work was of such a superb nature that his window displays for the Brenda Department Store attracted huge crowds of people whenever he worked. Barton Frisbee was an artist. He might have been a Michelangelo or a Rembrandt—how practiced his fingers were! How skillfully his hands moved and designed and created—so that each of his three mannequins came to life with each new dress design, each current fashion trend. His admirers were legion. His window for the Easter season drew a breathless crowd of women who watched him work. It was curious because Barton Frisbee was by no means pretty. He might have been Hugo's Quasimodo—he was so ugly. And like the weird bell ringer of Notre Dame, he was a hunchback and nearly a ludicrous sight as he scampered among his tall plaster and

wax mannequins with bolts of material over his crooked
arms.

But there was beauty in Barton Frisbee. And the
beauty was in his creations for the windows of Brenda's
Department Store. And nobody laughed at him. Not
until one terrible morning in May. The windows had
been stripped clean in preparation for some more of
Barton Frisbee's creativity. There were two tall mannequins waiting to be dressed in summer styles. The motif
of the window was *Fun in the Sun—Let Brenda's Dress
You for the Summer*. The props were a beach ball and
umbrella, papier-mâché sand banks. Barton Frisbee
hunched through a tiny door at the rear and entered
upon his stage. The window lights beat down. A crowd
of curious passersby had already gathered. The great
Frisbee was ready to work.

Fascinated, the mob watched while the ugly, hunch-
backed man went into his act. They saw him dress the
models, one female and one male, in summer wear. A
polka dot playsuit for the woman, matching trunks and
sport shirt for the male. It was wonderful to behold.
But suddenly, the candy-striped beach ball rolled,
brushed against the female figure and toppled it. Barton
Frisbee's back was to the thing and suddenly the crowd
was laughing uproariously and pointing, trying to at-
tract his attention. Barton Frisbee had always been
oblivious to the crowds because people were cruel,
people knew how to wound and hurt. But now he felt
surprise and turning, saw what had amused everyone
so much.

The female mannequin had fallen against the male
and both had fallen against the false front of sand

banks. It was strange indeed. The arms of the models had been so built that they now seemed to be embracing in some form of communion. Laughter beat against the windows. In the mad heat of the scene, Barton Frisbee stared at his models, looked at Vivian, his Vivian. Locked in the arms of the handsome Tod.

You see—he had always had pet names for his models. They were real to him. Not dead figures of plaster and wax. And now Vivian had become a woman like all others. A flirt, a plaything, a toy for the attractive male. The crowd stopped laughing. A small child, nose pressed to the window, began to cry in a tortured whimper. Because the funny little man with the hump on his back had sprung forward with a prodigious bound, torn the locked models apart, and was doing something terrible with the big, shining scissors in his gnarled hand.

Repeatedly, over and over again, Barton Frisbee stabbed the points into the female mannequin's body. The windows rang with the maddened outcries of a soul in torment. The crowd hushed—chilled—terrified. Only a dummy, you might say. Just a thing of plaster and wax. But red ran out of the stabbed figure. Before the frightened eyes of a score of witnesses. And something else too. Barton Frisbee had gone insane—ripping, tearing, screaming at his displays. And when he stumbled over the outstretched legs of the male model, Tod, and fell forward on the twin points of the scissors in his fingers, who could question the hand of Fate? So Barton Frisbee died where he had lived. In the window of his art, his place of genius . . . but I shall show you something in the window just over here. Look . . . see that

tall wax woman standing in the corner? See how beautiful she is. Ash blonde hair, perfect features . . . but
look at her eyes. Observe closely . . . do you notice
the *expression* in them . . . ?

Tom, Dick and Horror

The story of the Jones brothers

Do you know what fear is? Naked fear? It is the razor's edge between life and death—the tick-tock heartbeat when you poise dangerously on the dark ground between sanity and insanity—reality and unreality. Unlike Never-Never Land, it is something we all come to know at one time or another in our waking lives. Fear. Naked fear. It is an ugly thing to see in the faces of three boys no older than sixteen. Let me tell you the weird tale of Tom, Dick and Harry. And the night when they encountered naked fear . . .

Deep in the darkest part of the Witches Woods, a mile past the country town of Greenville, is a clapboard shack of wood and grass. You might laugh if you come upon it suddenly because it is so ramshackle and helter-skelter. But the boys who built it and formed the strange club known as The Wood Pirates take themselves very seriously. Greenville is a dull town where nothing ever happens and the boys of the village could not resist the chance to have their secret meeting place in the woods —their secret society that parents might frown on if they knew about it. The more owls that hooted and the strange cries of nearby animals made everything so much more scary and spooky and fun. And there were initiations—what fun—bringing in new members!—

teaching them the rules, and making them sign their names in their own blood on the charter.

Like the night when the three boys were sworn in. The Jones brothers, Tom, Dick, and Harry, had just moved to Greenville so it was fitting that they should become members of The Wood Pirates immediately. The brothers were led blindfolded through the woods by the Chief Pirate and his men. The door creaked as they entered the shack. Someone lit a candle and everybody formed a tight circle with Tom, Dick and Harry in the center. The Chief, a tall, thin boy with freckles, read the rules. The Jones brothers took their oath and their blindfolds were removed.

Then each in turn pricked his wrist with a safety pin and scrawled his first name in blood on a long sheet of parchment. Then a hush fell over the group and the Chief Pirate solemnly declared that a final test had to be made and the initiation ceremonies would be complete. Tom, Dick and Harry felt a chill sweep over their young bodies. What would this test be? They would soon find out. The Chief ordered all the candles in the shack to be snuffed out. In the darkness a silence fell over the gang of boys. Then the Chief's voice could be heard. He began speaking in a properly terrible voice of doom.

"Oh, brothers of the Order of The Wood Pirates—we have three new brothers who seek to join us. This is good. But first—the final test—Tom, light your candle and tell us what frightens you the most."

Tom shakily lit his tallow, his young face bobbing in its light and said he was afraid of fire. Then the

Chief's voice urged his brothers to do the same—one by one. Another match struck, another candle glowed and Dick huskily admitted he was afraid of water. Still another candle lit and Harry, the youngest brother, confessed that of all the things he feared the most, it was cemeteries. Oddly, only the three faces of the brothers were visible in the room. And then quite suddenly, the candles wavered and blew out—and somebody screamed. Loud and terribly . . .

The tale would have no meaning except for a few curious incidents. You can never get a coherent story from any of the other members of The Wood Pirates. No one can explain just what happened when the three candles blew out. The boys had all fled in terror during the screaming. And no one has ever asked the Chief what kind of test he was going to put the Jones brothers to but . . . on the very next morning, Tom died in the blazing inferno of his jalopy when it fell into Carlyle Canyon; Dick drowned in Stillman Lake a few miles away. And late that evening, Harry was found in Grove Cemetery, sprawled across a headstone near his family plot . . .

Now, possibly there is a logical explanation . . . had the Wood Pirates pushed their initiations to the extreme? But the Jones boys were alone at the time of their deaths . . . at least . . . nobody *meant* anybody to die . . . or was it just naked fear showing itself in the face of the three boys?

Come, I see my story has disturbed you . . . but we must continue with your initiation . . . if you want to be a member of the Graveyard Watchers, you'll have

to be made of sterner stuff. Remember the rules . . .
you are to be in the center of Grove Cemetery at
twelve midnight on the dot . . . now you promise not
to run if you see or hear anything . . . don't you?

Portrait in Hell

The story of Robert Roeburne

Come with me to an auction. A very strange auction. It isn't far. We must hurry—for today the Farron Studios are auctioning off the canvases of Robert Roeburne. Surely, you must have heard of the Great Roeburne? No? Here, we'll take this taxicab, and I'll tell you about the demoniac artist whose stunning work in oils has baffled the art experts to this day . . .

Robert Roeburne was English and, fittingly enough he won his greatest fame in England. Possibly because they are a conservative people and Roeburne's work was anything *but* conservative is the explanation for his striking, sudden fame. We think of the English as people who putter in green gardens in quiet Surrey; so many tea-sippers who like plain, normal, everyday living. But Robert Roeburne's work must have ignited the slumbering, passionate spark for the outre, the out-of-the-ordinary that is in all people. His canvases were splashing, dazzling studies in oil that were brushed with the frenzy of a madman.

The thematic quality alone was startling. He depicted scenes of Salem witch burning, a Black Mass at fabled Stonehenge, the strange pile of Druid rocks that is a monument to mystic mankind; London Bridge and the Tower of London were scenes from Hades shown as no tourist has ever seen them. Robert Roeburne's fame was electric and compelling. But it was also highly controversial. The students hailed him as a true great in the best traditions of the Old Masters. The churches and the old age groups were frightened by him and therefore loud in their denunciations. But Roeburne prospered and his fame spread around the world.

And one stormy day in his work studio in his mountain home on the lofty cliffs of Dover with the seagulls hawking in the leaden sky, Robert Roeburne began what was to be his last painting. He was alone before his easel, the great fireplace behind him roaring with the sound of blazing logs. The room was warm and dulling but Roeburne liked to work with a fire going. He prepared his oils and paints and set a large, blank canvas on the board. And then his brush moved in his fingers. Slowly, forcefully, his arms and hands worked with a steady, full rhythm. He painted long and hard and soon the daylight no longer streamed through the big glass windows of the studio. The storm had increased in fury. Angry seas of dark sky boiled and roistered outside. But Robert Roeburne worked on and a full five hours later, he halted and brushed the perspiration from his eyes. Exhausted, he fell into a big chair by the fireplace and looked at his latest creation with burning, almost feverish eyes.

Had you been there, you might have had that feeling that you had been present at the birth of something terrible yet wonderful. The firelight seemed to play over the painting. Robert Roeburne had painted the *Devil*. And Roeburne's devil was a fiend incarnate. The canvas throbbed with brilliant reds of deep hues and the twisted body and grotesque face it framed fairly leaped out of the canvas into the observer's eye. Roeburne was pleased. This was the Devil indeed. Spiked tail, horned head—but the face was *life* itself. The lips were curved and cruel, the nostrils flaring and sensual; the eyes deep and mocking and mad. And the artist had done the unpardonable. Satan's face was a full-blooded caricature of Robert Roeburne laughing and howling at his world of proper, mundane critics. It was Blasphemy in Paint of a high order.

And that's exactly what Roeburne called the painting. He had charcoaled the title in at the right-hand corner of the canvas. But Robert Roeburne fell asleep. Deep, tormented sleep . . .

And when they broke down his locked studio door the next morning and his frightened servants rushed into the room—the art world had a mystery that has not been solved to this day. You see, Robert Roeburne was in his chair by the fireplace. He had died in a sitting position—but how oddly! His body was dressed in a long flowing cape; his feet were encased in curved moccasins. And the skullcap on his head was devilish. As was the mustache and short, spiked beard he had grown. His face was twisted and mocking even in death and the glaze of his dead eyes held cruelty.

A pity. A real pity. Because the painting propped on the easel was a handsome, subtly glowing self-portrait of Robert Roeburne. Quiet, austere, dignified —a truly magnificent study of a great artist . . . Here— we are just in time. The bidding is on already. Why, look . . . it's the canvas I've told you about . . .

Blasphemy in Paint . . . you'll bid for it? . . . excellent!
But a word to the wise is sufficient, my friend . . .
the Latins had an expression . . . *caveat emptor* . . .
which means . . . buyer beware!

The Graveyard Nine

The story of the Ravenswood Rangers

Terror knows no one particular country, no native ground. Nor does it discriminate against men because of their race, color or religion. Terror has invaded all countries, all homes, all professions . . . and possibly therein lies the lawful fright of Terror. Now, would you ever believe that Terror could infiltrate upon the placid, green fields of baseball? Come, sit yourself beside me and look out upon the playing field while I tell you the eerie and uncanny history of the Ravenswood Rangers . . . a baseball team like no other.

It was just last summer in the little railroad town of Melville. And it was the occasion of a night baseball game between the league-leading Melville Hawks and the second place Ravenswood Rangers. The rickety wooden stands of the ball park were jammed with white-shirted fans and flag-waving children. Cries of soda vendors and popcorn merchants filled the night air. Giant spotlights played across the field, illuminating the wire fences, the stands and the quiet green of the diamond with its chalk foul lines and anchored bases. But the fans were impatient. It was already eight o'clock and the starting lineups had been announced but the home team, the Melville Hawks, had not taken the field as they should have. Which was odd to say the least. The crowd could see the players in the dugout, standing impatiently, nervously punching their gloves and staring toward the big exit gate in center field. What had happened?

Soon, the answer to that question was visible to all. A large, grey bus pulled up to a stop near the exit gate and uniformed players piled out rapidly. A huge *boo* went up from the crowd. The Ravenswood Rangers were late! Laughter raced through the packed stands. A whole ball club late for a game! All Melville roared its laughter.

After the initial ceremonies were dispensed with, Melville took the field and the Rangers took their first at bat. Possibly it was the long bus ride but—the first three Ranger batters didn't swing at a single pitch and the Melville pitcher recorded three strikeouts. The crowd hooted derisively and the Hawks came in and Ravenswood took their positions in the field. Each of them looked tired and spiritless and their subsequent play showed it. Melville went on a tear and piled up five big runs before the third out was made. It was a curious game indeed.

As the innings wore on, the newspaper men in the press box behind home plate shook their heads. It would be a slaughter. The Rangers just couldn't seem to buy a base hit. They shuffled out to their positions with drooped shoulders. Not one ballplayer spoke to another. None were shouting or whooping it up. The Rangers' infield was almost solemn. Their lack of team spirit was atrocious. The crowd, sensing this woeful sportsmanship, got on them with a vengeance. It made the game dull. Even though the home team was winning, even though the scoreboard showed twelve runs for the Melville Hawks and a glaring 0 for the visiting Rangers at the end of the seventh inning, nobody felt like rejoicing. It was a terrible game—as if a grownup had whipped a child half his size.

But the game wore on. And suddenly someone in the press box woke up to the fact that not one Ranger had gotten the semblance of a base hit! The Melville pitcher was hurling a no-hitter! But the shabby play of the Rangers had detracted from the performance. And when it was the ninth inning and the last Ranger batter stepped up to the plate with his team trailing thirteen to nothing, the ball park was as silent as a grave. There was nothing left to cheer about. The Ranger batter took three called strikes and the ball game was over. And the crowd was still booing as the Rangers walked to their bus behind the exit gate in center field and drove off in a grey cloud of dust.

No one in Melville ever forgot that ball game. Because as the crowd was filing disconsolately out of the ball park, the wireless in the press box tapped out the tragic news: A bus loaded with baseball players had crashed through the safety railing of the bridge at Melville Crossing and disappeared into the river, killing all on board. Yes—the team *was* the Ravenswood Rangers. But the tragedy had occurred at *seven o'clock* that very night—a full hour *before* the fiasco of a ball game in Melville.

Why are you so frightened? Oh, that team out there?
No—they're alive, all right. Unless, of course, they
had an accident *too* . . . on the way out to the ball
park . . .

Say Good Night to Mr. Sporko

The story of William Welles

There are things that happen to us in our infancy that never can quite be explained. How many times have you wondered and pondered about something that occurred many years ago? Something for which your adult mind can make no explanation? Oh, you can visit the psychiatrist and he'll blandly say you had too much ice cream that night—or possibly you mixed pickles with milk. But—judge this particular tale for yourself. It happened to William Welles when he was only ten years of age. And the same thing happened every night when Mr. Sporko came to visit his parents . . .

The Welles home was a quaint little cottage on the Surrey Road in England. Mr. and Mrs. Welles were a couple devoted to the occult and mysterious. Their home was a veritable shrine of Buddhas and Sivas and ancient deities. Strange paintings and carvings of long-dead civilizations hung from every wall. But to their small son, William, the house was a wondrous playground. To his childish eyes, the Welles home was a riot of color and design. It was almost like the carnival that came down the Surrey Road once every year.

And on Saturday night, an hour before midnight, Mr. Sporko would come. Funny little Mr. Sporko with his black coat and bald head and shiny glasses. Mr. Sporko always visited the Welles' on Saturday night. And little William looked forward to his coming. Because Mr. Sporko always had a bag of jelly beans and funny stories for little William.

But then the clock would approach twelve and Mother Welles would get up, clap her hands and smile: "Say good night to Mr. Sporko." And William would dutifully rub the sleep out of his eyes and toddle upstairs to bed. And the big living room door would slide shut and William would go to bed eternally wondering what Mr. Sporko and his parents did after he had gone to sleep. He never saw Mr. Sporko leave either. Oh, many was the night he tried to stay awake to see the funny little man depart but always it became late and he was fast asleep in his bed before he could watch Mr. Sporko go. And so it went for a whole year. Come Saturday night, Mr. Sporko would arrive, play with William until close to midnight and then Mother Welles would urge her son to "say good night to Mr. Sporko" and the fun would be at an end.

"Say good night to Mr. Sporko." It became almost a litany to little William. The words would puzzle around in his head until he fell into sleep. And then in his mind the thing grew. Like all small boys, William Welles had to find out for himself. So one Saturday, he made plans and followed them through with great cunning. He ate lightly all day, napped for the better part of the afternoon. So when Mr. Sporko put in an appearance, he was well rested. Mr. Sporko's bag of jelly beans were thrust in a pocket untouched. Finally, Mr. Sporko and Father Welles went into the living

room and Mother Welles said, "Say good night to Mr. Sporko," again. William dutifully did and marched upstairs.

But when the big living room doors rumbled shut, he stealthily crept back downstairs and eased himself up to the oaken doors. William's heart beat like a tom-tom. He was only a small boy, you see, doing something he knew he shouldn't. A strange flurry of voices sounded behind the closed doors. William drew closer. He was on the eve of the greatest discovery of his life. Now, he would know what went on while he slept in his room upstairs. Slowly, eagerly, he inserted his small fingers in the crack that separated the doors. Gently, silently, he drew them inches apart. The strange voices picked up in volume. Light streamed out from the inner room and William Welles, aged ten, peered in . . .

Perhaps like the psychiatrist you'll say what he saw was a small boy's vivid imagination or a bad diet . . . or fever . . . but William Welles saw a scene from Hell . . . Mr. Sporko was dressed all in black; his bald head gleamed with a crown of roses. Mr. and Mrs. Welles were kneeling before him in blood-red robes, their heads flung back while Mr. Sporko read aloud from a massive, black book. But far more terrible— the room was thronged with people. Strange people in still stranger clothes. People with faces like skulls; thin, haunted spectres of the graveyard. William Welles screamed and fainted . . .

There would be nothing more to the tale except for the simple, irrevocable fact that William Welles never saw his father and mother again. Or Mr. Sporko. It was as if the earth had swallowed them up. And no one ever believed the poor little orphan's tale about the mad party he had witnessed when he peered through the living room door . . . well, that's all there is to the story . . . but before you retire . . . won't you say good night to Mr. Sporko . . .

Beware the Bird

The story of Monah Trent

The bird of death flies high, spreading its black wings over the world. See how it wheels in flight! First this way—then that, its dark shadow blotting out the earth below. The wings of death blanket us all until that final, inevitable day when we stand directly beneath its shadow. Keep your eye on the sky while I tell you the weird, unbelievable tale of Monah Trent. And the bird in her life. A bird more ominous than The Raven . . .

Monah Trent was a spinster. Old before her time, cold and loveless. She lived in the old family house on Elm Street. She was a lonely woman; unmarried, childless and friendless. Her one companion was her bird— a pet canary named Blue Boy. The years came and left with only Monah Trent and the bird occupying the bleak old house on Elm Street. The Trent neighbors shook their heads and wondered at Monah. It wasn't right, they said, that a woman of only forty-five should shut herself out from the world with nothing but a canary for company.

But Monah Trent didn't think Blue Boy was nothing. She loved her little bird with his yellow coat and the odd blue streak running across his body. Blue Boy was her one consolation in life. She would talk to him intimately; all her secrets became his. There was nothing about Monah Trent that Blue Boy did not come to hear. He was almost like a person listening as she cooed to him while he pranced in his cage—the cage whose door was always opens so Blue Boy could fly about the house whenever he desired.

And one fine summer morning, Monah Trent burst into her house and rushed to the cage. She was all aflutter and Blue Boy could sense the new feelings working in his mistress. Monah Trent poised Blue Boy on her finger and told him all about it. The new school teacher, handsome Mr. Benning, had asked for her hand in marriage. Think of it! Someone was in love with her—someone wanted *her* for his very own! And what's more, she had accepted him. She wanted him too, and now the bleak world seemed like a sunny place after all.

But Blue Boy reacted strangely to the news. He made a noise in his furry throat and flew off Monah Trent's finger and sailed aloft to the highest point in the room above the fireplace. He refused to come down despite all his mistress' pleadings. But Monah Trent was so happy, she did not see the tiny tear welling out from the bird's left eye.

The following days were all the same. Monah rushing in and out of the house, buying new dresses, making frenzied plans for the approaching wedding. She sang to herself in the house, waltzed about the rooms with a phantom partner and ignored Blue Boy completely. She was a different woman. Love had touched her with its magic wand. But the same love that is so wonderful for some people is the thing that destroys others. Blue Boy, unobserved, unpetted and uncared for, languished in his silent cage all the time. No longer did he chirp. His happy whistle had gone stone quiet. And Monah Trent did not hear the awful silence that filled her home.

The morning of the wedding came and leaving her bridesmaids in her bedroom, Monah Trent came down the long, winding staircase to preen before the huge, oval mirror in the drawing room. She looked beautiful as all women do on the day they are to be married. But Blue Boy reacted violently at sight of her before the mirror. Suddenly he shot like an avenging angel out of his cage, and alighted on her cheek, pecking furiously, savagely. His sharp bill beat a vicious tatoo on Monah Trent's face. Blood gushed from her ivory cheeks. Terrified and frantic, she pawed Blue Boy away from her face and flung his tiny body to the stone sides of the fireplace. There was one piercing wail of a soul in torment. Then the big room was deathly still save for the racked breathing of Monah Trent. She walked slowly to the fireplace and knelt beside the crushed, pitiful little bird on the floor. The blood from his body stained the pure white of her wedding dress . . .

Monah Trent *never did get married* . . . when her anxious bridegroom reached the house to look for her, he found her by the fireplace cradling Blue Boy in her lap as if he were a child, stroking his bloody coat . . . she was quite insane after that, you understand . . . there wasn't a doctor in the world who could convince her that she hadn't *murdered her lover*. Curious tale is it not? But true. Do you know when Monah Trent died a year later and they buried her on the hill beyond town, a bird flew over the grave. Yes—a canary. Yellow body with a colored streak across its stomach. But the streak wasn't *blue* . . . it was *red*. So keep your eyes on the sky, my friend. When *your* bird of death approaches—make sure you stay out of its way . . .

The Phantom Soldier

The story of Captain Troy

Death is one of the Four Horsemen . . . those grim, gaunt, spectral night riders that make of all the world a bridle path. But Death is far more constant than his three ghastly companions. And nowhere do his hoofbeats pound more times, nor does his horse rear and scream so endlessly as it does on the battlefield of a world war. The ride of Death is long and constant and his figure ever present when men pit themselves one against the other. Listen to this tale of Death and of the ride of the deadliest of the Four Horsemen . . .

It was in the German village of Bardenburg just outside the walls of Aachen where so many Americans fell in battle. The advance of the American army had been diligent and unrelenting. Tanks, troops and artillery had pushed forward driving Hitler's divisions farther back behind their own lines. The German army was retreating and victory in Europe was becoming something more than an idle American dream. But there was still more fighting and more work to be done. And no one knew it better than Captain Troy of the mechanized cavalry. The Captain was the guiding force of a troop of the best trained servicemen—his outfit was dedicated to reconnaissance—the seeking out of the enemy.

Reconnaissance—dirty, bloody work for any soldier. It meant constant patrols, constant vigil. Being on your toes because all the territory you went into was virgin and deadly. It could mean a mass movement of your vehicles and men into an unreported position that might be crawling with machine gun nests or mortar squads. It could mean a squad of ten men on foot pressing on into enemy territory looking for some sign of enemy occupation and resistance. Just like tonight. Just like the squad of Sergeant John Browne.

Captain Troy had sent Sergeant Browne and his squad of ten men out on a reconnaissance patrol. But that had been five hours ago. And sitting alone in his command vehicle, Captain Troy was worried. Browne had taken his radio with him and should have reported in at ten o'clock. It was now eleven. Captain Troy kept looking at his watch impatiently. The night was black and depressing. Captain Troy's uniform clung to his body with sweat despite the chill of the night air. Sergeant Browne was a good man—he'd hate to lose him. All the way in from Le Havre, B Troop had been a successful, winning combination because of men like Sergeant Browne. Captain Troy smoked one cigarette after another from his ration pack. But the radio in his car remained silent. And the hour and minute hands on the GI watch on his wrist crawled slowly around to midnight. Finally, he heard a noise off in the brush.

Startled because he was half-dozing, Captain Troy swung the car lights on and shouted, "Who goes there?" To his great relief, the voice answering back was Sergeant Browne's. Happily, the captain walked toward the figure that stumbled toward him. Then shock replaced the relief he felt. Sergeant Browne was alone. He wore no helmet and his uniform was blood-smeared and in tatters. Captain Troy helped his squad leader to the car where he poured him some water from a canteen. And Browne babbled out the terrible story of what had happened; the squad had walked into an ambush at position X on the map. A machine gun nest. And all nine of the men with Browne had gone down. The sergeant had been barely able to make it back. But the patrol had served its mission—the Germans were in force at position X and now Captain Troy could call for the necessary artillery to destroy them.

He radioed his report in and then called a corpsman to attend to Browne's wounds. But when the medic arrived and saw Browne, he stared at the captain incredulously. Captain Troy exploded with anger and demanded to know what the medic was waiting for.

"Captain," the medic said. "If this is a joke I don't care for it. This guy's been dead for at least three hours." Grimly, Captain Troy turned his flashlight on Sergeant Browne . . . and saw at least fifteen bullet holes stitching their crazy design across Sergeant Browne's chest . . . but the blood was all congealed and dried . . . and Sergeant Browne's stiffened body was already cold . . .

So you see, Sergeant Browne was a good soldier. He reported back to his commanding officer . . . from the grave . . . John Browne's body received a medal it so richly deserved . . . posthumously of course . . .

Some Things Shouldn't Be Seen

The story of Hugo James

Have you ever wondered about your neighbors in a big city? You know what I mean. You walk the streets every day brushing shoulders with perfect strangers and you never know a thing about them. Or perhaps you move into a furnished apartment and live there for years without ever seeing or knowing the person who lives in the room right next to yours. A simple wall separates you from him or her but you never encounter anyone in the hallway or on the stairs. Now suppose you were Hugo James and you resided in one of those brownstone houses in the West Eighties in New York and you lived next door to a stranger. A stranger whom you only knew by the name of Tarbox . . .

Hugo James had a tiny room at the north end of the hall. The apartments were so situated that the door of the adjoining room was directly at right angles to his. The key locks were inches apart which had a curious effect on Hugo James. Many times alone in his room, he could hear his next door neighbor scratching at his own lock and it would sound as if he were keying James' door. At first it had startled Hugo James because it always seemed as if someone were forcing his way into the tiny room.

But no. The card on the downstairs bell said TARBOX

and even though Hugo James had never seen Mr. Tarbox, he had come to learn much of Mr. Tarbox's habits. It was always a few minutes to midnight that the scratching sound would begin and Hugo James would know that his neighbor had come home. It was easy to tell that Mr. Tarbox was a man because his footfalls on the other side of the wall were heavy and ponderous. Also, Mr. Tarbox was a drunkard. Hugo James would often hear him stumbling and falling over things until there was one final heavy crash and then silence. And Mr. Tarbox would stir no more until morning. Oddly, Mr. Tarbox's noisy tenancy of the next apartment did not annoy Hugo James as it might have another man. New York was so cold and friendless to Hugo James and the apartment house so deathly still that he welcomed the noisy presence of Mr. Tarbox. It was the sound of life and Hugo James was a shy, meek man who would never have dared to strike up an acquaintance with Mr. Tarbox. That is until one dreadfully rainy night when the wind and the storm beat against the building with a vengeance. It was nearing midnight and from force of habit, Hugo James put the book he was reading aside and waited for the sound of Mr. Tarbox's key fumbling and probing at the lock on his door.

Strange, now that he thought of it, he had never heard Mr. Tarbox coming up the stairs. But before he could pursue the thought further, a dull, metallic clinking sounded at the door next to his. Hugo James smiled. Mr. Tarbox was punctual as always. As regular as clockwork. But the scratching of the key persisted longer than was usual. Mr. Tarbox must be less sober than usual. Fiinally, Hugo James could endure that probing key no longer. Also, he had emboldened himself to the point of no return—now he could meet and see Tarbox. Now he could make friends with his next door neighbor. And possibly, his dull, lonely existence would come to an end. Eagerly, almost joyously, Hugo James approached his own door and flung it wide open . . .

He would better have minded his own business . . . he would better have stayed in his own world and not stepped across the threshold of madness and darkness and terror . . . Hugo James screamed. Screamed as no mortal has before or since . . . because crouched in front of the door next to his was a terrible, monstrous, scabrous entity.

A hunched, demoniac nightmare creature with claws for hands, blood-red lips drawn back in a fiendish leer exposing pointed horrendous teeth. Giant bat wings fanned out from misshapen shoulders. And even now, the wings were still flexing as if from some recent flight in the stormy night . . .

The landlady found Hugo James the next morning . . . he was spreadeagled by the stairwell, his throat torn out; his eyes two pools of terror. Hugo James, you see, had come face to face with that which *shouldn't* be seen . . . but wait . . . what's that deliberate knocking at your door? If you're not expecting company, don't answer it . . . Mr. Tarbox disappeared from his room the night Hugo James died so terribly . . . and you wouldn't want to meet Mr. Tarbox . . . *would you . . . ?*

You Can Take It With You

The story of Danny Denning

Come, my friend. Take my hand and walk with me in the darkness. It's so lonely now and cold. The streets are wet and unfriendly. Perhaps we can share the solitude together. And if you are of a mind to listen—I will tell you a very strange story indeed. The tale of a lonely taxicab driver and a midnight fare that came upon him as suddenly as I have encountered you. The cab driver's testimony is incontestable. He has the proofs of his weird experience. But enough of this— listen for yourself and judge for yourself.

Danny Denning had been a cab driver for five years and had encountered many strange people on his job. A cab driver, because of his occupation, does get to meet just about everybody sooner or later. And so it was on the night of August 30. Danny had just left a fare at the corner of West 149th Street when he heard a shrill whistle. He braked his cab to a halt to allow a tall, thin man with a parcel under his arm to get in. Danny was tired. The day had been long and wearisome and fate had decreed nothing but long runs and many passengers. It had been a profitable day, certainly —but Danny Denning was exhausted and there was to be no surcease from labor. The tall, thin man settled back against the cushions and gave an address in the Bronx that meant miles and miles of driving.

Danny sighed wearily, thumbed his flag down and hunched over the wheel to keep from falling asleep. In the rearview mirror, he could barely make out the face of his gloomy-looking passenger. The man was dressed all in black; his face was white in the dim interior of the cab. It was only the manner in which he clutched the parcel to his breast that aroused Danny Denning's flagging interest. The parcel must be something really valuable indeed. The way the man was holding it you would have thought it was a box full of rare gems or a fabulous invention.

Danny grunted and paid attention to the road. Street signs and store fronts and houses flashed by. Soon the city proper was far behind them. Danny probed his memory. The address given was familiar—he certainly knew where it was—but a tiny bell in his mind kept ringing. But he couldn't place it. The meter rapidly toted up the fare. And still the man in the rear said nothing—did nothing—but grip his parcel and stare straight ahead. And then Danny Denning slowed his cab. This was the name of the street given to him but the number—it couldn't be. Suddenly he realized that his cab was far from the city, far from life—that he was rolling slowly down the long dirt road that ran parallel to the big cemetery that filled acres of Bronx countryside.

Danny turned to ask his fare a question but to his surprise the man said, "This will be fine. Stop here." Dumbly, Danny applied his brakes. The cab was halted directly before the big, iron gates of the cemetery. And now Danny could see the number on the stone archway —the number his fare had given him. Tombstones and headstones shone dully in the darkness behind the front gate lights. But the man was alighting from the cab and thrusting a five dollar bill in Danny's hand. Before Danny could ask him anything more, the man had strode purposefully through the gates and disappeared . . .

It was strange, of course . . . but just another adventure in a cab driver's life . . . except for one thing . . . when Danny Denning reported back to the cab depot, he found his last fare's wallet on the back seat . . . and turned it in to Lost and Found . . . and thought no more of it. Three days later, Lost and Found sent a letter to Danny explaining to him that the wallet belonged to a John Adams who had died on August 28 and was buried in a Bronx cemetery . . .

Danny Denning checked his fare sheet . . . it had been August 30 when he had driven the tall, thin man to the cemetery address . . . the parcel? Well, my friend, possibly when we die there is something we want to take with us when we leave this mortal coil . . . and our relatives forget to bury it with us . . . who can really say what was in that mysterious parcel? Unless of course, you'd really like to find out for yourself. Come . . . the cemetery is just around the bend . . . I know the plot of ground . . . and I have a shovel . . . *will you join me . . . ?*

Children of the Devil

The story of Astra Vale

A woman's face sometimes can be a terrible thing. There is beauty in a woman's face; love can lie in the deep vibrant eyes; the full red mouth may hold tenderness and compassion. But a woman's face which can be all things to all men can also be the face of evil incarnate. Satan can hide behind the fair-skinned façade of a woman's beauty. Have you ever heard the weird and bizarre tale of Astra Vale . . . the loveliest woman that ever lived? No? Then listen . . . there's something here for all of us . . .

Astra Vale was not always lovely. Indeed—in the little village of Innisfree, a green jewel set down in the breathtaking hills of Ireland, no child was born uglier. Her little face was gnarled and crooked, her lips overly thick. She was not a pretty baby at all. Her sainted mother crossed herself fearfully and made daily pilgrimages to the church beyond the hill and prayed to God to set her child aright. For the first years of her life, no one ever set eyes upon Astra Vale. Her widowed mother was too ashamed to show her ugly offspring to her friends.

One windy day, Astra Vale, aged eleven, scampered into the heather in search of a lost ball. There she met the silent man who led her to a dark cave and invoked

the powers of darkness over her. The child was awed
and when the dark stranger disappeared and Astra returned home, her mother almost collapsed at the sight
of her. For a glow surrounded her child. And the
gnarled, twisted face was a thing of the past. Astra Vale
was now serenely beautiful—great majesty glowed on
the little face. Mother Vale crossed herself—her pray-
ers had been answered. And from that day forward,
Astra Vale's beauty became almost legendary in the
town of Innisfree. For miles around, she was the celebrated girl of that part of the country.

The years flew by and the vibrant, lush magnificence
of Astra Vale's face kept pace with Innisfree's history.
And one day, she was eighteen and at least fifteen
men would have gladly swum the Channel just for a
look from her. But nature took its normal course and
Astra Vale lost her heart to Tom Reilly. The wedding
day was a big one—a roaring, noisy happy occasion for
everybody. And Tom Reilly and Astra Vale tripped
happily to the little cottage that Tom had built with his
own hands in the valley.

All Innisfree waited for the fine line of offspring
their union would bring forth. But history, fatal history,
repeats itself. One night, almost a year later, Astra
bore Tom Reilly a son. A frightening, terrible, hideous
son, and her anguished screams filled the cottage. And
when Tom and the midwife had quieted her down and
taken the baby from the room, Astra fell into a troubled
sleep. But she awoke soon to the sound of logs crackling
in the fireplace—and the dark stranger was standing in
the center of the room. Astra recognized him immediately from her childish memories of the windy after-

noon long ago. And when she asked the stranger what he wanted, his mocking answer brought forth her worst fears and suspicions . . .

"I gave you beauty," the stranger said. "Unforgettable beauty for the price of bringing Satan's children into the world. And you cannot break your bargain." With that, the stranger vanished in a cloud of sulphur and fire. And Astra Vale lay terrified in bed all through the night, pondering and torturing herself for a solution. And when dawn poked through the windows, she knew what she had to do.

Carefully she got out of bed, walked over to the mirror on the wall and stared at herself. She saw the gleaming wonder and beauty that was the face of Astra Vale. Then closing her eyes, she picked up her sewing shears and steeling herself, drove the sharp points into her own face over and over again . . . They still talk about Astra Vale in the little town of Innisfree. Because, you see, in spite of her terrible accident, her face bears not the slightest scar and she is as lovely as ever . . . too bad that her child died that very morning but she's still a young girl . . . and there's lots of time yet . . . tell me, my dear, would you make such a bargain with the Devil just for a face that would drive men mad . . . ?

THE END